D0175139

Dear Parents and Educators,

Welcome to Penguin Young Readers! As parents and educators, you know that each child develops at his or her own pace—in terms of speech, critical thinking, and, of course, reading. Penguin Young Readers recognizes this fact. As a result, each Penguin Young Readers book is assigned a traditional easy-to-read level (1–4) as well as a Guided Reading Level (A–P). Both of these systems will help you choose the right book for your child. Please refer to the back of each book for specific leveling information. Penguin Young Readers features esteemed authors and illustrators, stories about favorite characters, fascinating nonfiction, and more!

Young Cam Jansen and the Circus Mystery

LEVEL **3**

GUIDED READING LEVEL **J**

This book is perfect for a **Transitional Reader** who:
• can read multisyllable and compound words;
• can read words with prefixes and suffixes;
• is able to identify story elements (beginning, middle, end, plot, setting, characters, problem, solution); and
• can understand different points of view.

Here are some **activities** you can do during and after reading this book:
• Setting: The setting of the story is where it takes place. Discuss the setting or settings of this story. Use some evidence from the text to describe the setting.
• Creative Writing: In this story, Aunt Molly tries many different ways to make the clowns in the circus laugh. For example, she uses lipstick to paint red circles, squares, and triangles on her face. Pretend you are also trying to make the clowns at the circus laugh. Write a paragraph describing what funny things you might do.

Remember, sharing the love of reading with a child is the best gift you can give!

—Bonnie Bader, EdM
  Penguin Young Readers program

*Penguin Young Readers are leveled by independent reviewers applying the standards developed by Irene Fountas and Gay Su Pinnell in *Matching Books to Readers: Using Leveled Books in Guided Reading*, Heinemann, 1999.

For my friends Sara Rose, JaJa, Danielle, Sam,
Maayan, and Ben—DA

For Hannah Rose and Mason—SN

Penguin Young Readers
Published by the Penguin Group
Penguin Group (USA) Inc., 375 Hudson Street, New York, New York 10014, USA
Penguin Group (Canada), 90 Eglinton Avenue East, Suite 700, Toronto, Ontario M4P 2Y3, Canada
(a division of Pearson Penguin Canada Inc.)
Penguin Books Ltd, 80 Strand, London WC2R 0RL, England
Penguin Ireland, 25 St Stephen's Green, Dublin 2, Ireland (a division of Penguin Books Ltd)
Penguin Group (Australia), 707 Collins Street, Melbourne, Victoria 3008, Australia
(a division of Pearson Australia Group Pty Ltd)
Penguin Books India Pvt Ltd, 11 Community Centre, Panchsheel Park, New Delhi—110 017, India
Penguin Group (NZ), 67 Apollo Drive, Rosedale, Auckland 0632, New Zealand
(a division of Pearson New Zealand Ltd)
Penguin Books (South Africa), Rosebank Office Park, 181 Jan Smuts Avenue,
Parktown North 2193, South Africa
Penguin China, B7 Jiaming Center, 27 East Third Ring Road North,
Chaoyang District, Beijing 100020, China

Penguin Books Ltd, Registered Offices: 80 Strand, London WC2R 0RL, England

Text copyright © 2011 by David A. Adler. Illustrations copyright © 2011 by Susanna Natti.
All rights reserved. First published in 2011 by Viking, an imprint of Penguin Group (USA) Inc.
Published in 2013 by Penguin Young Readers, an imprint of Penguin Group (USA) Inc.,
345 Hudson Street, New York, New York 10014. Manufactured in China.

The Library of Congress has cataloged the Viking edition
under the following Control Number: 2010031961

ISBN 978-0-448-46614-9   10 9 8 7 6 5 4 3 2 1

ALWAYS LEARNING   PEARSON

Young Cam Jansen

and the Circus Mystery

by David A. Adler

illustrated by Susanna Natti

Penguin Young Readers
An Imprint of Penguin Group (USA) Inc.

Chapter 1
I Could Be a Clown

Cam Jansen's
aunt Molly stuck out her tongue.
She put her hands behind her head
and waved them.
"Aren't I funny?"
Cam, her friend Eric Shelton,
and Aunt Molly were in line
to buy tickets to the circus.
"I want to sit in the first row,"
Aunt Molly said.
"I want to make the clowns laugh."

"I want to sit high up," Eric said.

"I want to see the tightrope walker."

Cam closed her eyes.

She said, "Click!"

With her eyes still closed, she said,

"We can sit in the first row

for the parade.

All the clowns will be in the parade.

Then we can sit high up.

This circus lets us change seats."

"How do you know that?"

an old man in line asked.

Cam said, "The circus poster says
'open seating.'"

"But your eyes are closed,"
the old man said.

"Cam has an amazing memory,"
Eric told him.

"She has pictures in her head
of everything she's seen."

"What else is on the poster?"
the old man asked.

"In the middle is a clown," Cam said.

"At the bottom of the poster
are elephants, tigers, giraffes,
and monkeys."

Cam opened her eyes.

The old man said,

"You really do have an
amazing memory."

"When I want to remember
something," Cam told him, "I just
close my eyes and say, 'Click!'"

Cam pointed to her head.

"That's the sound the camera
up here makes."

Eric told the man, "Her real name
is Jennifer, but because of her great
memory, we started calling her
'the Camera.'

Then 'the Camera' became
just 'Cam.'"

"I have the tickets," Aunt Molly said.

"Let's go inside."

Chapter 2
Oops! Did I Step on Your Foot?

Aunt Molly, Cam, and Eric entered
a large hall.

"Get your circus programs here!"
a woman called out.

"Caramel popcorn!" someone else
shouted.

"Ice-cold water and soda!"
Aunt Molly bought an extra-large
box of caramel popcorn.

Then Aunt Molly, Cam, and Eric
walked into the circus arena.

In the center of the arena
was a large ring.
Around the ring
were rows and rows of seats.
"Let's sit in front," Aunt Molly said.
"The parade is about to begin."
The clowns led the parade.
Aunt Molly put the popcorn box
on her head.
She wrapped her scarf
around the box.
She tied the scarf under her chin.

"Look at my popcorn hat!"

A clown with a toy duck

on his head stopped.

He laughed and pointed to the duck

on his head.

"Quack, quack!" the clown said.

Aunt Molly pointed to her popcorn

hat and said, "Pop, pop!"

When the parade ended, a short man

wearing a big top hat came out.

"Welcome!" he called out.

"The show is about to begin."

"Let's sit higher," Eric said.

Aunt Molly took the popcorn box
off her head.

Then she and Cam followed Eric.

Eric stopped near
the top of the arena.

"Let's sit here," Eric called out.

"Excuse me," Aunt Molly said
to a large man with a small beard
at the end of the row.

"Oops, did I step on your foot?"

"Yes," the man said.

"I'm sorry," said Aunt Molly.

Cam and Eric walked very carefully past the man and his small son.

"Let them by," a girl sitting next to the boy told her mother.

"Look!" Eric called out, and pointed.

"Here come the dancing elephants."

The girl stood on her chair.

"Yeah!" she shouted.

She waved her cotton candy.

The cotton candy stuck to the boy's hair.

"Oops, I'm sorry," the girl said.

Cam and Eric ate some
caramel popcorn.

Then Aunt Molly closed the box
and put it under her seat.

A clown sped around the ring
on a tiny tricycle.

He was chased by a clown
in a police uniform.

"Look at that clown go!"
the girl shouted, and pointed.

When she pointed,

she knocked over her mother's cup.

Soda spilled on the boy.

"I'm so sorry," the woman said.

The man wiped the soda

off his son's shirt.

Eric saw the spilled soda and said,

"I'm thirsty."

"Let's get something to drink,"

Aunt Molly said.

"Please, excuse me," she said

to the girl and her mother,

and to the man and his son.

"Excuse me," Cam and Eric said.

Aunt Molly, Cam, and Eric hurried

down the stairs and outside.

Aunt Molly bought three bottles

of water.

Eric drank some water.

Then he said, "I'm going back."

Aunt Molly and Cam followed him.

"Excuse me," they said to the large

man with the small beard and his

son at the end of the row.

"Here come the jugglers," Eric said.

Two women dressed as bakers

juggled large loaves of bread.

Eric looked at the bread and said,

"Now I'm hungry.

I want some caramel popcorn."

Eric looked on the floor

next to his seat.

He looked next to Aunt Molly's seat

and Cam's.

"Where's our popcorn?"

Chapter 3
I Think I Know What Happened

"I left it under my seat,"

Aunt Molly said.

She looked under her seat.

She looked under Cam's and Eric's

seats, too.

"The popcorn is gone," she said.

The short man with the top hat

came out.

"Look to the high wire," he called

out, "for a great act of bravery."

A tall, thin man walked to the center
of the ring and bowed.
Then he climbed a ladder
to a small platform.
A long wire was attached to that
platform and to another at the end
of the ring.
The man tapped the wire with his foot.
The wire shook.
"Ooh!" people in the arena shouted.
The man carefully stepped onto
the wire.

He stretched his arms out to his sides
and slowly walked across the wire.
"I'm still hungry," Eric whispered.
"Sh," Aunt Molly told him.
Eric watched the tightrope walker
slowly walk to the other platform.
People in the arena cheered.
Eric looked at the man sitting
at the end of the row.

"Cam," Eric whispered.

"I think I know what happened
to our popcorn.

I need you to look at the picture in
your head of that man."

Eric pointed to the large man with
the small beard at the
end of the row.

"Did that man have a box of
popcorn when we left?"

Chapter 4
BAM!

Cam closed her eyes and said,

"Click!"

"Yes," Cam said with her eyes closed.

"He did have popcorn."

"Look!" Aunt Molly said.

"Here comes the cannon."

Clowns pushed a large cannon

to one side of the ring.

At its base was a long fuse.

"I bet I know what the man did,"

Eric whispered to Cam.

"He finished his popcorn and was
still hungry.
He took Aunt Molly's popcorn box
and put it in his empty box."
Two clowns brought out a ladder.
They set it by the mouth
of the cannon.
The short man with the top hat
came out.
"We end the show with a blast,"
he called out.
"Bullet Bob, the human cannonball,
will be shot into the air.

"Maybe he'll land near you."

A man wearing a silver cape

and a silver helmet came out.

He bowed, and people cheered.

Bullet Bob took off his silver cape.

He climbed into the mouth

of the cannon.

Eric whispered to Cam,

"We have to get Aunt Molly's

popcorn before that man eats it all."

Bullet Bob waved.

He slid down the mouth

of the cannon.

A clown lit the cannon's fuse.
Eric started walking toward
the man at the end of the row.
BAM!
Smoke filled the arena.
Small bits of silver paper
flew over Cam's head
to the highest parts of the arena.
Cam turned, but she didn't see
Bullet Bob.
She saw something else.
"Wait!" Cam called to Eric.
"Come back!"

Chapter 5
Another Parade

Eric walked slowly back.

"There he is!"

a girl a few rows back shouted.

"There's Bullet Bob."

Clowns danced around a huge bed

at the other side of the ring.

In the middle of the bed was

Bullet Bob.

"But that's our popcorn," Eric said.

"No, it's not," Cam told him.

"Our popcorn is three rows back."

Eric turned.

Under a seat three rows back was a

large closed box of caramel popcorn.

"How did it get there?" Eric asked.

"It was always there," Cam said.

"Look at the noisy girl sitting

in that row.

She's the girl we were sitting next to

at the beginning of the circus."

Eric looked at the girl.

Then he looked at the man

and his son at the end of their row.

"But he was sitting in our row, too,"
Eric said.

"He must have changed his seat,"
Cam said.

"Well, I'm still hungry," Eric said.

"I'm getting the popcorn.

Excuse me," he said as he walked

past the man and his son.

Then Cam asked the man,

"Did you change your seats?"

"Yes," he said.

"That girl kept screaming and

jumping.

She got cotton candy in my son's hair.

She spilled soda on him.

So we moved down a few rows."

Clowns marched into the center of the
ring, followed by dancing elephants.

"It's another parade," Aunt Molly said.

Aunt Molly opened her purse.

She took out a tube of red lipstick.

She painted red circles, squares,
and triangles on her face.

She puffed out her cheeks and looked
at the man at the end of the row.

The man and his son laughed.

"Let's go," Aunt Molly said.

"This time I'll make
lots of clowns laugh."

Aunt Molly and Cam started
down the steps.

"Wait for me," Eric called.

He was eating caramel popcorn as he
hurried toward Aunt Molly and Cam.

When Aunt Molly got to the edge of
the ring, she waved at a clown.

The clown looked at Aunt Molly.

Aunt Molly puffed out her cheeks,
and the clown laughed.

Cam and Eric looked at Aunt Molly.

They laughed, too.

A Cam Jansen Memory Game

Take another look at the picture on page 6.
Study it.
Blink your eyes and say, "Click!"
Then turn back to this page
and answer these questions:

1. Is anyone wearing a hat?

2. Are Cam's eyes open or closed?

3. What's written on the sign above
   Cam's head?

4. Is anyone wearing a blue striped
   shirt?

5. Does anyone have a mustache?

6. What color is Eric's jacket?